The Rancher's Gift is a fascinating and compelling tale that sure to show you a new pathway to deeper meaning and purpose in your life. Don't miss out on this compelling message.

—*Les Parrott, PhD, #1* New York Times *bestselling author of* The Good Fight

Our minds are wired for good storytelling, and Dennis Worden and Jeff Dunn are great storytellers! But beyond just being drawn into this terrific narrative, you will find the principles for life and purpose are spilling out of this book. You'll love it, and you'll be so glad you read it!

—*Clay Scroggins, lead pastor, North Point Community Church*

The Rancher's Gift will take your imagination on a wonderfully engaging journey, causing you to pause and reflect on life's biggest questions along the way. If there was ever a book that was worth the time it took to read, this is it.

—*Dr. Todd Cartmell, child psychologist and author of* 8 Simple Tools for Raising Great Kids

Heartwarming, inspirational, and real-world, *The Rancher's Gift* provides powerful principles for pursuing and achieving a successful life with purpose.

—*Lt. Col. Waldo Waldman, author of the national bestseller* Never Fly Solo must read, you'll find *The Rancher's Gift* to be a power-ul parable full of reminders and revelations that are life changing as you apply its truths.

—Julie Gorman, a John Maxwell certified coach,
author, and speaker

Dennis and Jeff do a masterful job of weaving the life of a rancher with powerful illustrations and application into God's timeless truth.

—Boyd Bailey, author of Wisdom Hunters *devotionals*
and founder of Wisdom Hunters, Inc.

The Rancher's Gift is very compelling. Couldn't wait to turn the page and learn something more!

—Jennifer Du Plessis, principal and CEO,
Kinetic Spark Consulting

If you want to live ON PURPOSE, read *The Rancher's Gift*! This powerful modern-day parable by Dennis Worden and Jeff Dunn can change your life.

—Tim Enochs, executive coach and New York Times
bestselling author of On the Clock

Inspiring and heartwarming, *The Rancher's Gift* is filled with timeless truths and serves to remind us of the trans-formative power of relationships.

—Dr. Randy Ross, founder & chief enthusiasm officer
of Remarkable! and author of Remarkable!

Intricate and beautifully written, this is a captivating book about the journey of uncovering purpose and maximizing potential.

—*Dr. N. Cindy Trimm, international conference speaker, former senator, and bestselling author*

No matter your age, *The Rancher's Gift* will leave you fully equipped for success, true fulfillment, and living a life on purpose.

—*Dr. Sam Chand, author, speaker, leadership architect, and change strategist*

This amazing story will make you realize what is most important in life. It isn't the cash, the cars, or the house. A father's love will reach deep within your heart as he gives his son the greatest gift he can give—the gift of tough love. *The Rancher's Gift* brings us a wonderful story of life balance, love, loss, and courage.

—*Laurie Calzada, entrepreneur, TV host, author, and international speaker*

Dennis and Jeff have a strong commitment to family, integrity, and investing in the next generation. This book, *The Rancher's Gift*, takes a refreshing look, through the mentoring of The Rancher, at living on purpose.

—*Stan Reiff Sr., CPA, CGMA, professional practice leader, consultant, CapinCrouse LLP*

The RANCHER'S GIFT

The
RANCHER'S
GIFT

A Modern
Day Parable
of Living
a Life on
Purpose

DENNIS WORDEN
and JEFF DUNN

BroadStreet
PUBLISHING

BroadStreet Publishing® Group, LLC
Savage, Minnesota, USA
BroadStreetPublishing.com

The RANCHER'S GIFT
A Modern-Day Parable of Living a Life on Purpose

ISBN 978-1-4245-5648-9 (hardcover)
ISBN 978-1-4245-5649-6 (e-book)

Stock or custom editions of BroadStreet Publishing titles may be purchased in bulk for educational, business, ministry, fundraising, or sales promotional use. For information, please e-mail info@broadstreetpublishing.com.

Cover by Chris Garborg at garborgdesign.com
Interior by Katherine Lloyd at theDESKonline.com

Printed in China

18 19 20 21 22 5 4 3 2 1

Dedicated to all the "ranchers"
who have been examples of what it means
to live a life on purpose.

1

The first time Ryan Westcott heard the term *big sky*, he thought it was just some advertising cliché meant to lure unsuspecting visitors to the barren lands of Montana. He had been here only once before when he was fourteen years old, coming with his mother to visit her brother James, a rancher who was too busy, or so it seemed, to travel to see his sister in Pennsylvania. That is, until he had to come for Ryan's mother's funeral two years later. Even then, the rancher only stayed two days, and barely ten words passed between Ryan and his uncle.

That was ten years ago. Ryan wondered if he would notice the big sky this time. When he came here before, Ryan was expecting to see cowboys wearing six-shooters at their hips and having gunfights in the center of the street. He was disappointed to learn that neither his uncle nor his cousin wore gun belts, and they drove a four-wheeler more than they rode horses. "It's faster to get where I need to go," said Uncle James when asked why he didn't ride his horse out to repair a fence gate. "Got too much to do to waste any time."

Apparently, wasting time to James Royale included attending Ryan's college graduation, though he did get a nice gift that he figured Aunt Helena had picked out.

And then a card, signed by Aunt Helena for their whole family, when he received his MBA two years later. Ryan was proud of that degree—it was earned at Wharton, after all—and a number of doors had opened for him because of that. But the only door he wanted to walk through was the business his dad had built and was offering to him, if …

That is where our story begins.

"The sizzle might be in new technology," his dad had said so many times, "but the steak is in the way business has been conducted for thousands of years—by moving one thing from here to there." Ryan's father had started with three trucks and two drivers when Ryan was in diapers; he now moved more freight in the Midwest than all but two other companies. When Ryan was an undergraduate at Penn State, his father branched out into wholesale fuel supply and delivery. It was this part of the business that he had promised to Ryan, and for which Ryan had spent the last two years at Wharton working hard to prepare to take his place in what he figured would be his life's work.

Then, a week after receiving his MBA diploma, the floor dropped out from under him. Ryan had already begun to move his stuff into an office his dad had cleaned out for him and was actually hanging his diploma when his father knocked on the open door and came in. "Want some dinner?" asked Peter John Westcott, better known as PJ. "Stop what you're doing and let's go eat."

Ryan and his dad were seated in the back of a small Italian bistro, a place Ryan knew well. It was his mom and dad's favorite restaurant for the few times they could get away by themselves. PJ had not been here since his wife had passed away, and Ryan was surprised his dad chose this place tonight. He was even more shocked by what his father had to say in between their salads and the main dish.

"I'm not going to let you come to work for us, Ryan," said PJ. "At least, not yet."

Ryan looked at his dad, wondering if he was pulling

3

his leg. Yet he knew that look on his dad's face, and there was no humor in it.

"What do you mean? I thought we had agreed … you told me … what do you mean?"

PJ looked at his empty salad plate, took a sip of his wine, and said, "You're not ready. Or maybe a better way to put it is that I haven't made you ready."

Ryan sat in stunned silence. His first thought was of the Wall Street job he had turned down the month before, the six-figure salary with the very real potential to make it seven figures in a matter of time. He had aimed all along to come into the family business—his dad had all but promised it would be his one day—and now … and now?

"I want to tell you something, son," said PJ. He paused as the server delivered their next course. "I thought I was a good husband and father. I built a successful business, was making a lot of money. I could afford to buy you and your mother nice things. But …" He let the word hang in the air. "Remember the summer you and your mother went to Europe? I think it was between your sophomore and junior years of high school, wasn't it?"

"Between freshman and sophomore years, dad," Ryan said.

"Okay. But you remember the trip? You and Mom spent two weeks in Europe, and by all accounts had a great time. Where was I? Why wasn't I with you?"

Ryan remembered the trip as if it were yesterday. His mother had just received the news from her doctor that the cancer she thought was in remission had recurred. She wanted a family trip before she began chemo treatments. PJ said he was too busy to take off two weeks, so Ryan went alone with his mother as they visited Italy, France, Spain, and England.

"She pretended she wasn't upset, said she understood." Ryan saw tears running down his dad's cheeks. Once Ryan and his mother had returned, the doctors told her the cancer had spread too much for chemo to do much good. She had two rounds of it before she died in the fall of Ryan's sophomore year of high school.

"I was—am—a good businessman, Ryan. But I wasn't—and still am not—a good father. I could hand you this business, a multi-million-dollar business that is built for growth for many years to come, and I have no doubt you would run it and run it well. I could do that right now, but I'm not going to."

Ryan looked up from his plate with anger and confusion in his eyes. "And why aren't you going to do what you said you would do?"

"Ryan, if I do that, I am sentencing you to a life where you will think everything comes easily and naturally to you. You will not be a good father, just as I wasn't a good father to you."

"What do you mean?" asked Ryan, a spark of anger rising up in him. "I never said you were a bad father."

"No? Then how many of your baseball games did I ever attend?"

"Dad, I didn't play baseball."

"Exactly. Nor did you play football or soccer. You made the freshman basketball team, but then you quit because you said you didn't like it. You said you didn't like all that practice just to sit on the bench. We had a hoop in our backyard. How many times did I take you out to shoot? Go on, tell me."

Ryan picked at his lasagna with his fork. He remembered when he and his dad had put up the basketball hoop in their backyard. They were halfway through a game of one-on-one, playing to ten, when his dad got a call. "I'll be right back," he had said. Ryan could not think of one more time they played any game together again. That half-finished basketball contest lay before him now, making him feel sick. He pushed away his plate.

"I never encouraged you to play sports, Ryan, partly because I had never played them much myself, partly because I didn't want to see you fail, but mostly because of the time commitment. I would need to help you practice, go to your games, and all of that would take time away from my business. So I let you stay inside and watch TV and play video games. Your mom argued that with me, but I didn't listen. I had my own world I was living in."

"What does that have to do with me going to work in the job you promised to me? You promised it to me, Dad. I've turned away other offers so I could work here, with you."

Ryan's father looked at him for a long minute, opened his mouth, then said to himself, "No. Do it." He looked at his plate, pushed it away, and said, "I want to do something for you that you may not understand, and you may not like, but that I know is the best thing for you. I want to

"I am confident you can run
a business. But that is not all that
goes into being a man. God made you
to be more than just someone who
makes money. You were made to help
build and shape the lives of others."

make up for the lousy job I've done preparing you to be a good husband for my future daughter-in-law, a good father for my grandchildren. It sounds clichéd to say I want to help you become a man, but there it is. That's what this is all about. I am confident you can run a business. But that is not all that goes into being a man. God made you to be more than just someone who makes money. You were made to help build and shape the lives of others. I want you to be more than I am, Ryan. I can't undo all the mistakes I've made. But I can do better now, and that's what I'm trying to do."

Ryan was too shocked to process all his dad was saying. He didn't even have a girlfriend, so why did he have to think about being a good husband and father? And what did God have to do with this? His mom was the one who had taken him to church while his dad worked half-days on Sundays. They had never really been a religious family, and Ryan thought this was a bad time to introduce the subject of God.

"So what do you want me to do, Dad?" He spit out the words, not trying too hard to hide his anger. "What do I have to do to earn my 'man card' and impress you?"

PJ smiled for the first time that evening. "Now, I'm glad you asked that. I do have a plan. And remember, I said I didn't want you to come to work for me *yet*. If you will do as I ask you, your job—and your office—will be waiting for you."

Ryan felt a bit of the frustration and fear he had been feeling for the last half hour start to recede. A bit. "What kind of plan?" he asked.

PJ took another sip of his wine and said, "What do you remember about your Uncle James?"

Once again, Ryan's world tilted. He hadn't thought of his uncle in years. And what could that cowboy have to do with him?

"I don't remember much. I never understood why he didn't come here much and we didn't go there if he was family. But I didn't give it much thought, to be honest."

"That's a good enough answer," said PJ. "I suppose James didn't come here or invite us there because he didn't think much of me. He loved your mother—he loved her a lot. They were as close as brother and sister can be. He was two years older than her, but because their father died when your mom was still in high school, James became like a father to her. He even walked her down the aisle when we got married. But when he looked at me, he didn't, well, he didn't see much that he liked. James is old-fashioned. He believes people need to earn their stripes."

"But Dad, you earned your stripes! You built your business from the ground up."

"Yes, but like I said, James is old-fashioned. He sees that there is a lot more to life than just business. And son, he's right. So I called James last week and asked him if he would be willing to help me do what I should have done all along as your father. I asked him if he would help me make you who you were made to be."

2

"The sky still seems just as big as ever," Ryan said from the passenger seat of his uncle's pickup. His ears still buzzed from the puddle-jumper he had taken from Chicago to Bozeman, but the scene before his eyes was all he could think of.

"Sun rises in the east and sets in the west here just like everywhere else," said Uncle James. He was a big man and looked cramped in the cab of the truck. After another minute, he added, "I suppose we do tend to take the scenery for granted 'round here. I don't count those puny hills you have back East as mountains."

Ryan's eyes fixed on the mountain range surrounding them—they reached up to the endlessly soaring sky.

"I'll bet you've never seen the Milky Way or the northern lights, have you?"

Ryan gazed around him as he answered. "Well, no, I guess I haven't."

"That's because you have too much else going on where you live. All of those buildings and city lights crowd out the things you should be noticing."

Ryan was quiet, partly because his uncle intimidated him and partly because he felt an awe coming over him, a sense that he should show respect with silence. Everything seemed larger-than-life here. When he glanced to his left, he realized he felt the same toward his uncle. James was someone to be respected, someone to heed.

"And apparently you can't see other things that are important because you've let business and schooling and such crowd them out. I think that's why your pa wants you to spend some time here. He's hoping your eyes will clear up, and you'll see the stars."

The back of Ryan's neck heated with anger, the same as two weeks earlier at the Italian bistro with his father. He said nothing, fearing that if he did it might spark an argument with a man he hardly knew.

Finally, James spoke up again. "Your Aunt Helena is back at the house, baking you a cherry pie." James looked up and down at Ryan, then said, "Though it appears to me you've been eating plenty of pie. Haven't missed too many meals, have you?"

Ryan sat up a bit straighter in his seat. "I do need to get back to the gym. I've not had much time to work out lately."

James gave a bit of a snort. "There aren't any of those fancy-dude gyms out this way. We 'work out' by working. We don't have a lot of things you're probably used to back East. We don't put flavors in our coffee, we don't have any restaurants whose chefs have their own TV shows, and we don't have gyms where you can show off your latest hundred-dollar sneakers. I'm not sure you'll like it here, even for the summer."

They rode in silence for a bit, then Ryan asked, "What about pretty girls? Are there any of those around?"

Uncle James grinned. "Maybe one or two. Not sure you're ready for them yet."

"Well, maybe they're just not ready for me." Ryan laughed.

"There's Kayla. Now she's a fine girl. She and Hank have been best friends since, well, grade school I suppose.

They have an understanding between them, though I'm beginning to wonder if Hank is ever going to get around to asking her The Question."

"How is Hank?" Ryan hadn't seen Hank since he was here last.

"He's fine. He gets around pretty well now. Took him a long time to get over his surgery." Ryan's father had caught Ryan up on Hank before this trip. Hank, James and Helena's only child, was an all-state defensive end his senior year in high school. He had college scholarship offers from some big schools, including Wisconsin and Oklahoma. That is, until he tore up his knee in the state championship game. There went the offers for free schooling. Hank, who was a year younger than Ryan, had taken classes at Montana State and graduated with a degree in agricultural business. Now he worked with his dad to run the King Ranch with its sixteen hundred acres of grassland and more than eight hundred head of cattle.

"So," Ryan said, "just what am I going to do here with you in order to learn how to be a man?"

Uncle James shifted in his seat so he could look at Ryan and the road simultaneously. "Listen," he said, "I know your daddy told you that was why he was sending you here to me. But I'm going to tell you what I told him. I'm no philosopher, and I'm no teacher. I'm a rancher. I'm not going to pretend I know what it takes to tell you or anyone else how to be a man. I need someone to help me put up a barn. I told PJ I would take you on this summer to help me with this project, and if you learn anything along the way, that'll be a bonus. I expect you to work hard, just like any man, or woman for that matter, I hire. You'll be paid wages and be housed and fed. I wanted to put you in the bunk-house with the other hands, but Helena wouldn't hear of it, so you'll use the guestroom in our house and eat with us. Oh, and we start tomorrow morning. I recommend getting to bed early."

3

⁓

"Breakfast is on the table. Best come get it while you can. James'll be wanting to get started in just a few." Aunt Helena had come into his room, raised the window shade, and was gone, with the call to breakfast coming all in one breath.

Ryan stared out the window. A thin gray line spread out on the horizon, the only hint that sunrise was coming. Far from getting to bed early as his uncle had advised, Ryan stayed up talking with Hank and then texting friends back East. He seemed to have just drifted off when Aunt Helena came calling.

He swung his legs out of the bed, his feet hitting the bare wood floor. He missed his Ugg slippers. He wanted to take a long hot shower but felt he was probably expected downstairs soon. After pulling on his jeans and a Penn State

T-shirt, he followed the bacon scent to the kitchen. James and Hank sat at the table, silently drinking coffee—strong coffee. He could tell by the aroma. Slowly, they both tilted their heads up and eyed him like he was intruding.

"You look terrible," Hank said. "Didn't you like your bed?"

"The bed was fine," Ryan answered as he pulled out the chair and sat. "It's just that I wasn't in it long enough. I'm not used to getting up before the sun."

"Best get used to it," James said. "We get started early here. Eat your breakfast, and we'll get going."

Aunt Helena put a large plate filled with scrambled eggs, bacon, potatoes, melon, and toast in front of Ryan. "Butter's on the table, and jam is in that jar. Holler if you want more of anything—I fixed plenty."

"Uh," Ryan said. "You see, I don't really eat much for breakfast. I just grab some cereal or a bagel, then get a coffee on my way to wherever I'm going. This is, uh, a nice breakfast and all, but I'm not really that hungry."

Hank and Helena both glanced at James. Ryan's stomach lurched. He'd said the wrong thing.

James scowled and held his breath for a full three-count.

"Son, I hired you to work for me. If you're not healthy, you won't be able to keep up and do all I need you to do. Your body is a living machine. If you don't put the right amount of the right fuel into your body, you won't function as you are supposed to. Also, your body will need to recover its energy each day—that's why you need good sleep." James looked Ryan up and down. "And it wouldn't hurt to brush up close to a bar of soap and a razor."

Ryan, feeling the eyes of his aunt, uncle, and cousin boring holes in him, dug into his breakfast. When he had eaten enough that he thought would satisfy them, he pushed back his chair. "Thank you, Aunt Helena, for the very nice breakfast. I'm ready now, Uncle James, unless you think I should shave first."

"Nah, you'll be okay. You'll just get dirty again anyway."

The air outside was crisp and chilly. Ryan started to shiver. "It's colder than I thought it would be. It's supposed to be summer."

"You'll warm up once we get going." James pointed to a stack of wood off in the distance. "In the meantime, there's a jacket you can use in the four-wheeler."

They climbed into a John Deere ATV—Ryan first

putting on an old jean jacket he found in there—and drove a quarter mile to where the barn was to be raised. There they found several large stacks of wood. Ryan checked them out. "All this wood looks used, Uncle James. Are you sure this is what you ordered?"

James chuckled, seeming to know this would be his nephew's first impression. "You're like most people your age," he said. "You mistake 'new' with 'better.' And that's not the case here. Yes, this is the wood I ordered. It came from a farm back East—in your home state, as a matter of fact. It was a barn there for more than a hundred years. I got lucky when the owners sold the land to become an eye-sore shopping center. They were all too glad to make a few dollars and have someone haul the wood away. So I hired a couple of guys who knew what they were doing to take the barn down properly and ship the wood here."

James pulled out a blueprint and unrolled it on the back of the four-wheeler. "This is what it'll look like, what you and I are going to build. Are you ready to start?"

Ryan looked at the plans, then back at the wood. "I still don't know why you wouldn't want to get some new planks here locally. Wouldn't they be stronger?"

"The old wood embraced the
hard seasons and grew stronger;
the young wood has yet to do so.
Give me seasoned wood
any day over green wood."

James thought for a minute and then walked over to the nearest pile of lumber. He selected a two-by-eight and stood it upright. "See this board? It's more than one hundred and fifty years old as a cut board. Before that it was part of a tree for several hundred more years. This board has endured hundreds of harsh winters and brutal summers. It has seen countless winters, springs, summers, and falls. It has gone through times of drought and through floods. It is seasoned wood—it has survived many different seasons.

"If you bought green wood—wood freshly cut from trees—and put up a barn next to this one, guess which one would keep you cool in the summer and warm in the winter? Guess which would be constantly expanding and contracting in different directions, trying to find its way? The old wood embraced the hard seasons and grew stronger; the young wood has yet to do so. Give me seasoned wood any day over green wood."

Ryan gave his uncle a smile. "I think you're trying to teach me something more than just the nature of wood, Uncle James."

"Well, maybe I am." James shifted to face Ryan. "I'm

trying to teach you to embrace what life brings you, be it summer or winter, spring or fall. Don't run from hard times—embrace them as a way of making you stronger. Those who run from hard times are not fully alive, for life is full of hard times. This wood didn't go seeking hardship, nor did it strike off searching for fun and pleasure. It stood firm where it was placed and took all that life brought its way.

"The same goes for you. Find where you are supposed to be, then stand firm there. Don't run away when a storm comes, trying to find somewhere better. And don't wilt in the heat. Enjoy each season as it comes and know that no season lasts forever."

"Now, put on those gloves. It's time we got to work."

4

Two-plus hours later, James and Ryan were seated in the four-wheeler, drinking coffee James had poured from a thermos into plastic cups. Ryan had shed his jacket and rolled up his sleeves and, in spite of the brisk light wind, was wiping sweat from his brow.

"You know," Ryan said, "you were right about breakfast. I do feel like I've got more energy today. I could go for some more bacon and toast right now."

James nodded. "Ryan, you need to get your body into a rhythm. Life all around us has a rhythm. Birds know when to wake, when to eat, when to sleep. When they eat, they seek food that was made for them, made to help them stay in their rhythm.

"Even the ground has a rhythm. It works hard in the spring and summer to provide nutrients for the crops we grow, growls when we pull the crops out in the fall, and recovers during the winter in anticipation of the plow again in the spring. If it didn't freeze and recover in the winter, it wouldn't be able to do its job the next summer."

James' eyes rounded with kindness. "Your body has been in a rhythm but not a healthy one. It happens to a lot of college kids. You get used to staying up late, sleeping late, eating junk, and not getting good exercise. It makes you tired and unable to think clearly. I'm not trying to put you down. I'm just observing what I see."

Ryan took a last sip from his near-empty cup. "So you think I should go on some special diet and do more workouts?"

James frowned. "Those so-called 'wonder diets' are just hucksters trying to sell you something. Is it really that hard to figure out what to eat? Eat the food God made for you to eat that grows in the ground or comes from animals, and don't eat plastic foods that someone invented in a factory."

"But I thought too much bread and red meat was supposed to be bad for you."

"The food police," James sneered, "will have you running in circles. Today they say eggs are good for you and bacon is bad. Tomorrow, bacon will be a wonder-food that cures whatever ails you, and eggs will lead to an early death. Don't pay any attention to these kinds of stories. Eat real food, eat at the right times, and don't overdo it. That's what your body is calling for."

Ryan nodded slowly, letting the words sink in. What his uncle was saying was so simple and straightforward that it made sense to Ryan. He was much younger than his uncle, yet his uncle had run circles around him moving wood this morning. Maybe there was something to this.

"Uncle James, what do you mean when you say our bodies work best in a rhythm?"

"Let's get back to shifting that wood," James said, "and I'll tell you."

They began moving wood into various locations, yet Ryan's mind was not on the work but on what his uncle was saying.

"Each morning is like springtime for your body. It's new, it's awakening, just like the ground in the spring. It's a time for sowing. And like we add nutrients to the soil to help it produce a bountiful crop, we give fuel to our bodies with the right foods. Then comes summer, the heat of the day. This is

"Life all around us has a rhythm.
Birds know when to wake,
when to eat, when to sleep.
When they eat, they seek food
that was made for them, made to
help them stay in their rhythm."

when plants are doing their work. They need rain and sun. Summer for our bodies is from mid-morning until evening. We need water and food throughout the day to help us work.

"Then comes fall, harvest time. This is when we reap the benefits of our labor. In the evening we sit down to dinner with a satisfying weariness in our bodies. If we aren't a bit achy or the least bit tired, then I wonder if we really worked as hard as we could. After a good day's work, that piece of pie or dish of ice cream will taste really good."

"Let me guess." Ryan wiped his forehead. "Nighttime is winter, when our bodies lie dormant like the ground."

"You aren't as dumb as some might think." James grinned. "Yes, night is like winter. And just as we let the ground lie still during that season, so you need to let your body lie still. I know that's hard for you young folks to understand. You think the night is for partying. Then you sleep until noon, get up and eat a bunch of sugar, and try to be productive. That's not the way God made us to work though. You need to be in a rhythm, Ryan. And the sooner you get there, the sooner I won't have to be doing all the heavy lifting myself."

Ryan laughed at what he hoped was his uncle's joke and searched for the heaviest board he could find.

5

⁓

"Kayla's coming by for dinner." Aunt Helena cleared away their lunch plates. She eyed Hank. "She wants to meet your city-bred cousin."

"Hmmph," Hank grunted. "She's met city folk before. I think she just wants a free meal."

"Don't talk about your girl like that!" Helena scolded. "If you're not going to treat her well, I will. She's welcome at this table anytime." She glanced at Ryan. "You'll like Kayla. Real sweet girl. She's studying to be a nurse, you know. She and Hank have been dating for a long time now. Long enough that some folk are beginning to wonder if Hank has sense enough to marry her." She cast Hank a withering glare. "Not that he deserves her."

"I ain't in no hurry, and neither is she," Hank said. "She ain't going nowhere."

"That kind of thinking will leave you an old man with no wife." She folded a dish towel and laid it next to the sink. "And me with no grandchildren."

"Hmmph," Hank grunted again as he headed out the door.

Ryan wasn't sure what he was supposed to do right then, as James had driven into town to get some hardware. "Let me help you with that, Aunt Helena." Ryan picked up a towel and started drying the dishes his aunt had washed. "It doesn't seem right for you to have to do all the work while I sit and wait for Uncle James."

"Thank you kindly, Ryan. It seems at least one young person around here has learned some manners." Her smile made Ryan glad to be able to share in the work.

"Aunt Helena, do you think Hank and what's-her-name …"

"Kayla."

"Do you think they'll get married? You say they've been together for a while now."

"They have been together for a long while, at least as friends. But Hank takes her for granted. He thinks just because they have been going together for a spell, he can stop courting her. He'll soon find out that is no way to treat a woman. It may be that he'll have to learn that lesson the hard way."

Ryan dried a large serving bowl and put in in the cupboard where Helena pointed. "You and Uncle James seem to be doing well," he said, then wondered if it sounded patronizing.

"Yes, we are. Do you know why? It's because my James keeps courting me, even after twenty-eight years of marriage. He treats me like it was our first date every day. And he puts my wishes ahead of his. Do you know what this is called?"

Ryan glanced at her as she put a bowl in the sink. He wondered if it was a trick question. "Love?" he answered warily.

"Yes, love." Helena nodded matter-of-factly. "Love is putting others ahead of yourself. The Bible talks a lot about love, how real love is not selfish, does not demand to get your own way. James may not talk about religion much, but he shows it. He is constantly putting my whims and wishes ahead of what he wants to do. You just watch. He'll come home from the hardware store with some gift for me. That's just his way."

"But how do I get started?" Ryan asked. "I mean, what if I meet a girl and like her? How do I show her that I want to do what she wants instead of what I want?"

"You start right now, where you are. You don't have to wait until you meet a girl to be unselfish. What I'm saying goes for any relationship. Put all of your friends ahead of yourself. Practice giving whenever you're with someone. With enough practice, it will become second nature. It ain't easy, Ryan. We all look to our own ways and our own wants whenever we can. We have to practice putting others first."

As she was saying this, Ryan heard the front door open.

After a moment, James walked into the kitchen. "I got enough nails to get started," he said to Ryan. "So let's get going." Pausing, he turned at his wife. "Honey, I got you some new gardening gloves. I noticed yours had a hole in one of the fingers."

Helena winked at Ryan. "See? What did I tell you?"

~⌒~

Ryan and his uncle worked another three hours, starting the framing for the barn. When they had finished, they returned to the house where Ryan took a long hot shower and changed into his "good" jeans. When he came downstairs, he saw the only other person in the living room was a girl he took to be Kayla. She had her back to the west-facing window, and the sunlight made her glow.

Kayla Sparks was beautiful. That's all there was to it. Ryan had seen many good-looking girls, but beauty was something he had never noticed until now. Not thin but certainly not fat in any way, she looked, well, like the perfect woman. She glanced at Ryan and smiled, and Ryan felt his world begin to spin.

"Uh, hi," he said. "I'm Hank's cousin, Ryan. Are you Kayla?"

"Yep, that's me." She tilted her head. "Hank told me you were coming. Have you been here before?"

Ryan told her his story, how he had last visited his aunt and uncle more than ten years previous, how his mom had passed away, then how he had graduated from college, and how his dad had exiled him until he learned to be a man. He couldn't avoid the touch of bitterness in his voice.

"So, you're going to learn to be a man, then leave us and go back East to … what? Be a man in an office cubical?"

Kayla delivered this barb with a spark in her voice that lit a fire in Ryan, though he didn't know why it should.

His first reaction was a defensive one. "No, I'm going to … I'm not just going to leave here. I'm helping my uncle build a barn. I figure that'll be a good learning opportunity for me. And I'm not going to have a cubicle. For your information, I already have a nice office with a window and everything."

"Yes, with a window and everything," Kayla said mockingly but with laughter in her voice that kept Ryan's anger in check. "And does your window have a view of mountains?"

Ryan didn't want to tell her that his window looked out over a parking lot filled with trucks, so he attempted to change the subject. "What do you do?" he asked. "Hank hasn't told me where you work."

"Well, I can't say I'm surprised. I'm not so sure he even knows. Hank keeps pretty focused on Hank." Her voice trailed off for a moment, then she continued. "I was going to go to nursing school, but money is a bit tight at the moment. So for now I work at the clinic in town. I'm the office manager, receptionist, accountant, and janitor. Occasionally I do open heart surgery if there's a line." She and Ryan laughed.

"James may not talk about
religion much, but he shows it.
He is constantly putting
my whims and wishes ahead of
what he wants to do."

"I'll remember that the next time I need to have my arteries cleaned out. I'll bet you would make a great doctor."

"You think so? I always thought I would, but somehow …"

"Well, anyway, I'll bet you are the best office manager in this whole town."

"I thank you, Mr. Westcott." Kayla curtsied. "I'll be sure to move you up on the waiting list for that heart surgery."

During dinner, Ryan listened as Kayla caught the Royales up on town gossip, including who was close to giving birth.

"Twins again!" Aunt Helena clapped. "That woman constitutes her own population boom!"

She also mentioned who was on the downhill slide.

"Old Jake's lived a good life," James said about an eighty-five-year-old man in the last stages of congestive heart failure. "I'll be sad to see him go."

But Ryan wasn't paying as much attention to what Kayla had to say as he was to her very voice. It was soft, and yet it touched his heart in a deep way. He had never felt this way around a girl before. He kept glancing at Hank to remind himself that Kayla was spoken for.

A bowl of baked potatoes sat in front of him, and he picked it up to help himself to seconds when he saw there was only one potato left. "Would you like this last potato, Kayla?"

"Why yes, I think I will," she said, and resumed her story about poor Mrs. McGillicutty, whom it seemed had fallen and broken her wrist.

Ryan held the bowl so Kayla could scoop out the potato. As he set it back on the table, he caught Aunt Helena's eye. She gave him a wink. *Well,* Ryan thought, *maybe this "putting others first" thing wouldn't be so hard after all.*

6

"Ouch!" Ryan dropped his hammer and grabbed his thumb. "That's the third time I've done that!"

"A smart feller would've learned after the first time." James smiled. "You need to learn how to hammer a nail."

"I know how to hammer a nail." Ryan glared at his uncle. "It's just, it's just …" He rubbed his now black-and-blue thumb, searching for what to say.

"It's just you don't know how to hammer a nail." James took a piece of sandpaper from his pocket and tore it in half. "Here, take this sandpaper." He handed it to Ryan.

Ryan eyed it as if it were a skunk.

"What do I need with sandpaper, Uncle James? You don't expect me to sand these boards before we put them up, do you?"

"It ain't for the boards, Ryan. It's for your hammer. Take this piece of sandpaper and rough up the head of the hammer. That way the head will grip the nail, not glance off it. That is, unless you like hammering your thumb."

Ryan chuckled in spite of himself and took the proffered sandpaper. He did as his uncle suggested and tried driving the nail once again. This time, the hammer hit the nail and didn't slip off. Two more solid strikes and the nail was in.

"There's a lot more to driving nails than just rearing back and swinging with all your might, son."

Ryan knew it was best to keep working as his uncle taught his lesson.

"For instance, you're apt to be splitting the wood ever so slightly with these nails unless you blunt the tip first." James took a nail in hand, held it near the tip, and gave it a solid tap with his hammer. Then he turned it around and placed it against the board he was nailing in place. "Now the nail will drive the wood forward rather than causing it to split."

"That makes sense, I guess." He tried it with his next nail.

"Pick up that rock at your feet and put it on the pile of wood. Now, use that to blunt the end of your nail before you use it on the wood."

Ryan did as he was instructed.

"And don't drive the nail straight ahead," his uncle said. "Let it go in at a slight angle. That will get it to hold longer and stronger."

"How do you know all this?"

"I didn't always know it. I learned it after I thought I knew everything."

Ryan tapped in the nail at a thirty-degree angle. "Any more hammering tips, Uncle James?"

"Yes. Don't hammer a nail into a knot in the wood. You're just asking for trouble if you do that. That's where the wood is the weakest."

This all made sense to Ryan, who had never thought much about a better way to hammer nails. He began to think about all the other things he took for granted that might be improved if he took time to think them through. Then James spoke up.

"It's what you learn after you think you know it all that counts, Ryan. The schools get it all wrong. They make you believe that once you finish a grade, you have mastered those subjects. In reality, what you learn in school is simply a drop in the ocean compared with what you should learn the rest of your life. I know you have a master's degree, and I'm right proud of you for getting that. Not too many people can say they stuck it out in school that long. But the most important thing you can learn when you are young is how to learn."

"Aren't you making a big deal out of just how to hammer nails?"

James paused for a moment, then came over to where Ryan was about to drive his next spike. "Here, let me show you." He quickly blunted the head of the nail, then drove it into the wood in three swings of his hammer. "It's not hard if you will learn to do it right."

Here comes another lesson in manhood, Ryan thought. And he was right.

"About the only tool most people know how to use these days is the phone. Something goes wrong in their house, and they pick up the phone and call someone to come fix it. Then they pay that someone good money for something they could have done themselves if they had but stopped to learn how to connect a couple of wires or use a plunger or drill a hole."

"Or swing a hammer?"

"Or swing a hammer."

James leaned up against the frame of the barn. "The first thing you need to understand is what you want to accomplish. What is it you are trying to build or fix? This applies whether you are building a barn or a business. Or"—and here he gazed straight into Ryan's eyes—"a relationship, like a marriage."

"You wouldn't use a hammer in a marriage, now would you, Uncle James?"

"You would be surprised how many men try to do just that. When the only tool you have is a hammer,"—James picked up a nail and set it against the wood—"then every problem appears like a nail." He struck quickly and drove it—Ryan figured purposely—crooked. "Even if your job involves a hammer, you need to be sure to choose the right hammer for the job. How many types of hammers do you think there are?"

"I don't know," Ryan answered. "Two? Three?"

"I can name ten." He held up the one he was using.

"The most important tool you
can put in your toolkit in dealing
with people is learning to listen
to them. ... Learn to listen—
not just hear, but really listen."

"This sixteen-ounce claw hammer is one. There's the ripping hammer, the rubber mallet, the wooden mallet, and the ballpeen hammer. A soft-faced hammer, a tack, a drywall, and a mason's hammer. Then, of course, there's the sledgehammer. Only one of these tools is the appropriate one to use in the job we are doing right now. If you try to drive nails into this wood with any of those other hammers, you'll end up with a pile of beat-up wood, and you'll have to start all over.

"Most people today don't take time to think things through. They just act and react, then when it all crumbles around them, they shrug their shoulders and start over. That's why so many marriages don't make it these days. At the first sign of trouble, men grab their emotional hammers and wail away. And then when that doesn't work, they say, 'It wasn't meant to be,' and take their troubles into their next relationship."

Ryan thought for a moment. "You and Aunt Helena seem to always get along." While that didn't sound as deep as he wanted, he didn't really know how else to say it.

"Do you know when Helena and I began building our

relationship? It was before our very first date. I determined not to act like a raving lunatic but to respect her for who she was. I was smitten by her, but I decided I wasn't going to take from her but give to her. The proper tool for the job, as I saw it, was sacrifice. Giving of myself to her every day. It started on the first date. She said she liked Italian food, but there wasn't one in our town. So I used some of my saved-up money to buy extra gas for the car and drove her to the closest town with a decent Italian restaurant. She saw my willingness to put her first, and that was the beginning of where we are today."

They stood in silence for a bit, then James said, "I'll try to apply it where you are in your business. You are going to have people work for you, and people are, well, very unpredictable. And if you treat everyone the same, you will end up with a pile of beat-up wood. You can't use the same kind of hammer on everyone who works for you. So here is a tip for you. The most important tool you can put in your toolkit in dealing with people is learning to listen to them. God gave you two ears and one mouth for a reason. Learn to listen—not just hear, but really listen. Listen with your eyes as well as your ears. If you will do just this one thing, you will solve the majority of problems when it comes to dealing with others."

Ryan was about to say something, but James interrupted him. "We've done enough standing around for now. Grab your hammer. This time, hit the nails, not your thumb."

7

Ryan pulled the reins of his roan gently but firmly, coming to a halt very close to the spot he wanted. He sat almost straight up in the saddle, with his knees gripping the roan tightly. He hoped no one could tell this big horse still made him nervous.

"Not bad, Office Boy." Kayla smirked. "Especially since two weeks ago a sack of potatoes looked better in the saddle than you."

Ryan took off the Stetson his uncle had given him, "not to look like a dude, but to keep the sun from your eyes like a sensible person would," and bowed in his saddle. "Thank you very kindly, miss—" This would have been a much more confident gesture had the horse at that moment not taken two steps forward, causing Ryan to lose his balance and almost fall off.

Kayla laughed joyously. "Okay, so the sack of potatoes would have done that better! Still, you have improved. When you started, I could have sworn you didn't know a horse's tail from its mane."

An evening about two weeks earlier, when Kayla joined the family for dinner in their home, she asked if Ryan wanted to go riding with her.

"You mean on a horse?" he asked, half in anticipation and half in fear. Maybe more than half in fear.

"Unless you want to try to rope and saddle a goat," Hank said, barely looking up from a large piece of apple pie.

"Have you ever ridden a horse before, Office Boy?" Kayla asked. "I mean, other than the kind you put a quarter in at the grocery store."

Ryan would normally have become defensive, but coming from Kayla, he took it as, well, friendship. At least he thought she was being just friends. Or was there more to it than that?

"No," Ryan said, "but I'm willing to learn—if you're willing to show me how."

"Well," Hank said, cutting himself a second piece of

pie, "are you two going to just talk or are you going to ride? Ryan can have that roan in the barn. He's pretty tame as far as that goes. Broke him myself."

"Yes, Hank is very good at breaking things." The sparkle left her voice. "Like our date last night. We had planned to go to that concert at church for weeks, but only one of 'we' showed up."

"I said I was sorry, Kayla." Hank sounded genuinely remorseful for standing her up. "I was working on the hay baler and lost track of time."

"Well, next time you can take the hay baler on a date. C'mon, Office Boy. Let's go see if you know how to fall."

Ryan and Kayla went out to the barn where her horse, a Palomino she had named Daisy, stood saddled and ready to go. She walked past Daisy to a stall in the corner where a brown horse with flecks of white over its body stood quietly eating hay.

"This is Pony Boy," Kayla said. "I asked Hank if I could name him. I was reading *The Outsiders* at the time, and the name seemed to fit, so … Office Boy can ride Pony Boy."

"You know," Ryan managed to keep only a slight trace of defensiveness in his voice, "I do a lot more than sit in an office. My dad runs several large businesses, one of which is a trucking firm. Can you drive an eighteen-wheeler? 'Cuz, I can."

"No. I can't drive an eighteen-wheeler. I spend all of my time playing with dolls and putting on makeup for tea parties." With a swish of hair, she headed over to the horses. "Now, let's see if you know how to fall."

Ryan didn't know why she kept talking about him falling—that is, until he climbed into the saddle and, trying to show he knew what he was doing, pulled tight the reins. The horse shook from side to side, tucked its head as if to do a somersault, and then arched its back, flinging Ryan out of the saddle and nearly face-first into a pile of fresh manure.

"Well, that was graceful." Kayla helped Ryan to his feet. "I would recommend Helena's apple pie over that horse pie you almost ate."

Ryan, hot-faced and breathless, slowly stood up and leaned against the side of the stall for a minute. "Man, that hurt. What happened?"

"Well," Kayla's eyebrows scrunched together, and she half-smiled as she gazed at his sorry condition, "you grabbed Pony Boy's reins tight. That pulled the bit in his mouth, which made him uncomfortable. He sought the easiest way to feel better, which was to give you a ride on the air express. I guess you forgot to show the horse your MBA diploma."

Anger and embarrassment moved over Ryan. His first response was to jump back on the roan and say, "I'll show you!"—both to Kayla and to the horse. But then he remembered what Uncle James had tried to teach him about being humble and learning. Ryan gathered himself and looked at Kayla. "Can you please teach me how to ride a horse?"

And of course, Kayla did. She stopped teasing Ryan and showed him the proper way to get into the saddle, how to hold the reins, and how to grip the horse with his knees. They made a few short and slow circles in the corral, and when she thought he was ready, they went for a short trail ride. Ryan didn't fall off anymore that day, or any other day in the two weeks they had been riding together.

Now, two weeks later, they sat atop their horses and surveyed the vista before them.

"This land sure is beautiful." Ryan breathed in the cool evening air.

"I'll bet there are some nice views where you live," Kayla said. "It can't all be freeways and skyscrapers."

"Oh, for sure we have nice places in Pennsylvania. Especially in the fall. When the trees start turning, the hills look like they are on fire. But out here, well … it all seems so, I don't know, wild. Free." He gazed at the rolling clouds that seemed to go on forever. "All I've ever known was classrooms and offices and sometimes the small cab of a truck. I've kept focused on books and spreadsheets and never took time to lift my head to look around me. I've never seen nature as I do now."

"Maybe it's not just the nature." Kayla glanced at him. "Maybe you are seeing a different way of living. Maybe you are seeing a new you."

Ryan thought on this. "I'll have to admit, after being here with Uncle James and Aunt Helena and, well, you … how can I say this? I really don't want to go back to my old life. I want something new, something more real than the way I've lived."

Kayla nodded. "I do know what you mean. We always need to be leaving the past behind and pressing on toward a higher calling, the calling God has placed in each of our hearts."

"Jesus said he didn't come
to help those who were perfect
but to help those who know they
aren't perfect. To help those who
are spiritually poor. All you have
to do is ask him to help you."

"Somehow, when you talk about God, it doesn't seem—I don't know—fake. It seems like you and God are friends or something."

Kayla laughed and shook back her hair. "We are friends, Ryan! We have been friends since I was a little girl. I asked Jesus to guide me and to forgive me for the wrong things I had done. We have been friends ever since."

"I doubt you ever did anything wrong, Kayla. Me, on the other hand … well, I've done plenty of things most religious people would frown on. I'm not sure your friend Jesus would want to hang around with me."

"There's where you are wrong, Ryan. Jesus said he didn't come to help those who were perfect but to help those who know they aren't perfect. To help those who are spiritually poor. All you have to do is ask him to help you. He does all the rest."

They sat in their saddles for a long time gazing out over the vista. Finally, Ryan spoke up. "I really want to put the past behind me and set off in a new direction. I want to do what God, as you say, has placed in my heart to do. I want Jesus to be my God, my friend."

Kayla shouted a loud "Whoopee!" and danced her

horse around Ryan's. "That is the best news I've ever heard! Let me tell you, you've got a great adventure ahead of you!"

Ryan knew he had crossed over a great divide to a new land, one with endless horizons and blue skies. "I'm really getting to like this land, Kayla. It does something to a person, makes him feel different inside. It makes me feel, I don't know, bigger."

"Ryan, you just met the Creator of the universe. He is now living inside of you. Of course you feel bigger!"

"Yes, I can see that. And I'm really glad of it. But something about this land seems to be calling to me."

"C'mon, Office Boy. Let's head back. In a minute you'll start singing a cowboy song about little doggies or something." Kayla turned her horse back toward the stables, but Ryan sat staring at the land for another minute. Then he too turned back. They rode in silence, both lost in thoughts that neither could have imagined just a few weeks before.

8

"*I*'m going to loan you out today, Ryan." James pushed aside his breakfast plate. "The parson needs some help, and I think you would be just the one to assist him. I'll take you there as soon as I finish my coffee."

That meant in no more than thirty seconds, as his uncle could drain a mug of the hot black liquid in one gulp. Ryan hurriedly shoveled down eggs—his second helping—and began taking large bites out of his toast when Aunt Helena spoke up.

"Now James, don't rush the boy. Ryan, honey, take your time. The parson ain't gonna go nowhere without you. And James, you know gulping your coffee like that gives you gas."

Ryan stifled a laugh at that last comment, then as he

swallowed the last bit of toast, asked his uncle, "What kind of help does the, er, parson need? Do I need to take some tools?" He was hoping that his uncle would say that Ryan would be fixing something on his well pump or mending a fence, even though Ryan had never done either of those tasks. Ryan was feeling more comfortable with the tools they used each day in the construction of the barn and had even worked several days on his own when James had to run some errands. (And James only had to undo one section of a window frame that Ryan did on his own.)

"No, you won't need any tools. Only a pencil—and your brain. Ol' Wesley's got a pencil, I'm sure. You got your brain on today?"

Ryan grabbed a Farmers Co-op hat from the rack. "Yep. It's fresh back from the laundry. Nice and clean."

"Ah, then you really have been brainwashed, huh?" Hank reached for his third helping of ham.

Ryan had attended church a couple of times with his aunt and uncle, mostly to be polite. The beyond-middle-aged man they referred to as the parson, Warren Wesley, was not the kind of preacher Ryan was used to. The church he attended back home—well, when he had time to attend, which he had to admit wasn't often these days—was a modern place, with video screens, a rock band to lead the singing, and a preacher who really held your attention with his relevant stories, real-life applications from the Bible, and inspirational talks.

Warren Wesley, on the other hand, was pretty much a one-man band. His wife played the piano, and they tried to harmonize in leading the hymns, which were dry and dusty. And when he got up to preach, well, all he did was talk about the Bible and people who followed what the Bible said and how that was truly living. Yet the people he talked about all seemed to die horrible deaths for following the Bible. *Jesus needs a better PR campaign than this man is giving,* thought Ryan. He soon started coming up with excuses for not attending the services, and his aunt and uncle didn't press him.

"Parson, this is my nephew, Ryan. He graduated from business school back East, and I thought he might be able to help you find that money." James Royale wasn't much for spare talk when he could get right to the point. "You can drop him off at the Feed 'n Seed this afternoon. I'll get him from there."

"Thank you so much, James," the parson said. "I'm always grateful for the help you and Helena give to us. Marcia always puts great stock in you folks."

"Tell her we said hello, Warren. I'll see you in church on Sunday."

As James drove off, Warren Wesley invited Ryan into his small, modest house, explaining, "We've lived here since, oh, about 1995, I guess. It's not a big house, but there always seems to be enough room for those who visit. Would you care for something to drink?"

Ryan said water would be fine. He was expecting the parson to get a bottle of water from the refrigerator, but instead he took a glass from the cupboard and got Ryan water from the kitchen faucet. Ryan was taken aback by the simplicity of that. He couldn't remember the last time he actually drank tap water. Even at his uncle's house, they stocked their fridge with plastic bottles of water. Ryan belatedly thought that, of course, this preacher probably couldn't afford bottled water.

"I'm afraid I've got myself into a bit of a mess," the parson said. "I never was very good at numbers. I even get

Bible verses mixed up—my wife has to correct me from the front pew almost every Sunday."

Ryan chuckled and asked how he could help.

"Well, our church finance committee meeting is next week. But as I review the books, I seem to have made some kind of error. Here, let me show you." Warren Wesley brought a green ledger to the table and opened it to the last entry. "According to this, the church has a balance of $2,493.17. But when I checked with the bank, they said we only had $1,850 and some odd cents. This is going to make it look like I am slipshod with our financial records— or worse. Your uncle said you went to business school, so I thought …"

"Well, I majored in marketing, not accounting, but let's see what we can find." Ryan flipped back to the previous month's entries, where the amount had balanced against the bank's records. In just a few minutes, he said, "Here's your problem. You paid someone named Archie Goodwin $643 for, well, I can't make this out."

"Archie painted the interior of the church for us last month. And that's right, I did pay him that amount."

"But you listed it in the wrong column. You put it down as a receivable instead of something you paid out. If we correct that, you will balance to the nickel."

The parson peered over Ryan's shoulder at the ledger, moving his head back and forth over the page, trying to see where Ryan had made the change. "Well, like I said, I never was one with numbers. I know it's important to keep up on things like this, but, well, life always seems to get in the way."

"Oh, but keeping tabs on your money is so important. You want to know where it is coming from and where it is going. And when you have more money coming in than going out, that's when you turn a profit." He felt like he was lecturing in a Business 101 course in college.

"A profit, huh?" The parson grinned. "In my business, I suppose we measure 'profit' in something other than dollars."

"Oh, I hadn't thought … But still, Reverend Wesley, money is important, even to the church. If you could find a way to bring in more money, you could build a bigger church. If you put in a modern sound system and some video screens upfront, you would attract more people, who would naturally give more money. It's really the same as a growth cycle in business."

"But how would I care for more people? I like to visit with the sick and the shut-ins. And I enjoy having my mornings for prayer and preparing my sermons. Marcia and I enjoy our afternoon stroll. It sounds like this growth cycle you talk about would mean having to give up the things that make this pastorate so enjoyable."

"You would hire more ministers! Give them the responsibilities you don't want. Sure, a bigger church will bring on a few more challenges and headaches, but you just hire people to handle those for you. A smart CEO gets to where he doesn't have to involve himself in the day-to-day aspects of the business. He acts as a visionary, the man with the plan. He gets others to carry out the plan according to his design."

"That doesn't sound much like being a pastor to me. I got into the ministry to help people, not to get to where I don't even know the names of those who come to church. No, sir, that doesn't sound appealing to me."

Ryan paused for a minute. "Parson, if you don't mind me asking, do you have any money set aside for retirement?"

"Yes, money is important. It allows us
to do the things God calls us to do
a little easier. But not having money
allows us to see God
in clearer ways at times."

Warren Wesley shook his head. "All that Marcia and I make, we put back into the church. To own the truth, I've never really thought about retirement."

Ryan was shocked to hear this from a man whom he took to be closer to seventy than sixty. "Oh … well … that's unusual. See, in college I studied about financial management and planning and, well, I think it is, um, not so wise to not plan for the future. To put your money to the best use possible. I mean, don't you want to retire some day? You know, be able to put your feet up and relax?"

Parson Wesley gave Ryan a kind, compassionate look— like a father would a young son. "I see that money has gotten in your way, my son. It has clouded your vision of what is real. As for retirement, the reason I haven't thought much about it is that I think I have a pretty good life right now. I see no reason to quit doing what I'm doing.

"Let me tell you a story." And he told Ryan this story:

A young man was vacationing in Mexico. One day he strolled through a fishing village and saw a man mending his nets next to a small boat. The young man wandered over to him. "Have you just been fishing?"

"*Sí*," he replied.

"And how did you do today? Was it a good catch?"

"Oh, I caught enough for our dinner tonight."

The young man was confused. Here it was only ten in the morning, and this man was done fishing for the day? And he only caught enough for that night's dinner?

"Why did you stop fishing so early? You could catch a lot more fish—there's plenty of day left. Don't you want to catch more fish?"

"Why would I want to do that, *amigo*?" the fisherman asked. "I have caught enough for my family for the day."

"What are you going to do with the rest of your day?" the increasingly agitated young man asked. It went against everything in him to see someone not push himself to the limit when it came to work and earning money.

"Well, after I mend my nets and clean my boat, I will play with my children. Then I will take a *siesta* with my wife. After our dinner, I will go to town to see my friends. We will sit together, perhaps play a game of checkers, drink a little, laugh a lot. It is a good life."

"But you could be making so much more money!" the young man said. "If you fished longer in the day, you would have fish to sell in the market. And with the money you made, you could buy a bigger boat and hire helpers so you could catch even more fish and make even more money. Then you could buy a couple more boats, hire more help, and become a force in the fishing industry here. In time you wouldn't sell your fish in the market—you would sell directly to the processing plants and cut a better deal. Perhaps you would even open your own processing plant for all the fish your fleet would be bringing in.

"Then—and this is where it gets

The RANCHER'S GIFT

exciting—you could offer stock in your company. Maybe you would move to New York or Chicago to oversee your fishing empire. You would be responsible for hundreds of employees. Your long hours of hard work would eventually allow you to retire to the kind of life you wanted."

"Retire? What would I do if I retired?"

"Why, you could do anything you wanted! You could find a small village like this one where you could live. In the morning you could take a leisurely trip in your boat, then play with your grandkids, rest in the afternoon, and spend the evening with your friends."

Ryan grinned. "Okay, Parson, I get your point. You are already living the life you want. But you can't deny that money is important, and that even God expects us to make money. And the more money you make, the more things you can have and do."

Parson Wesley thought for a moment. "Ryan, I'd like to introduce you to the richest man in these parts. Let's go hear what he has to say regarding money and wealth."

9

*P*arson Wesley chatted as he drove along a dirt road in his Toyota pickup truck. "Tom Hayhurst was born in the very house where he now lives. His daddy was born there too. Hayhursts have been in Palmer since before it was Palmer. Some were hardworking souls, ranchers, farmers—there was even a preacher Hayhurst at one time. They also had their share of drunks, horse thieves, and lay-abouts. But all in all, they are a good bunch."

He drove at about twenty miles an hour. Ryan wondered if all elderly people drove slowly, or if this old truck was going as fast as it could. He glanced at the odometer and saw that it had gone over two hundred thousand miles. "Parson, one thing you could do if you had more money is buy a new truck."

Warren Wesley didn't take his eyes off the road. "Ol'

Betsy and I have traveled many roads together, young man. I don't think we are ready to part just yet."

Ryan thought about this man's affection for his road-weary truck, and something nagged at him. Could it be that newer and more expensive wasn't always better? But then the parson was talking again.

"Yessir, Tom Hayhurst is the richest man I know. I think maybe you'll be able to learn a thing or two from him, some things you didn't get from all your book learnin'."

Ryan and the parson rode the rest of the way in silence. Ryan was trying to picture what kind of house the richest man in these parts would build. Probably single story but sprawling. Certainly with a pool. And a guesthouse. Did he have servants? Did people still have servants? His uncle had two ranch hands who lived in a bunkhouse, but he didn't think of them as servants. They tended the cattle, mostly, and kept all the machinery running. This Hayhurst fellow probably had lots of ranch hands. Maybe even a butler to greet them at the door and then show them into the den, where Tom Hayhurst would be sitting behind a massive desk, overseeing his empire. *Yes, maybe he will be able to give me some insights into land management,* Ryan thought.

They turned down a smaller dirt road, only a single-lane path, and Ryan saw an old house off to the right. It was painted a bright blue, and despite its age, had the appearance of being very well-kept. *Probably the gardener's house.* But then Parson Wesley pulled right up to the house, stopped the truck, and got out. Ryan saw a figure sitting in a chair on the porch. He had on a flannel shirt and a flannel blanket rested on his lap. The man waved at the parson and said something Ryan couldn't quite make out. Apparently, he wanted them to visit, so Ryan got out of the truck.

"Howdy, Tom," the parson greeted. "Glad to see you. I brought a young man with me I want you to meet. This here is Ryan Westcott. James and Helena's nephew from back East."

Ryan made his way up the porch to greet the old man. As he did, he saw the man shift slightly in his chair, moving the blanket on his lap to reveal … nothing. There were no legs underneath the blanket. Only stubs about halfway down his thighs. Ryan fought to move his eyes back to the man's face.

"So you're the nephew James was telling me about. Sit

down, sit down. I hear you're learning some lessons while you're helping build a barn for James. Like how to swing a hammer without breaking your thumb." It wasn't said unkindly, but with a bit of sauce to it.

Ryan laughed in spite of himself. "Yes, sir, I'm trying to learn how to do things the right way."

"Tom, I told young Ryan here that he needed to meet you. Ryan was helping me with some of my books, and we got to talkin' about money. I told him I wanted him to meet the richest man in these parts. I thought you might be able to teach him a few things about being rich."

Now Ryan was really confused. Was this man, sitting here in front of a humble house, with a blanket covering up what used to be his legs, wealthy? The wealthiest man around?

"You'll be wantin' to know what happened to my legs, no doubt." Mr. Hayhurst's eyes reflected a passionate peace within him.

Ryan nodded, and so Tom continued.

"My wife, my daughter, and I were returning from a vacation in Colorado. We were no more than thirty miles from home when a drunk crossed the highway and hit us head-on. Lily and Carly died instantly. I was pinned in the wreckage for more than an hour before they could get me out. Amazingly, the driver who hit us walked away with nothing but a few scratches. But it sobered him up right quick. He took off running and hasn't ever been found. I wish I could meet him face-to-face. I want to tell him that I forgive him, so he doesn't carry this with him the rest of his life."

Ryan leaned forward. He wished he could help this man. "I'm sorry. I didn't know."

"I stayed in the hospital for two weeks, then I was moved to a nursing home for rehabilitation treatment. I thought I would die there. The parson here came to visit one day when I was at my lowest. I asked him why I should even want to go on living without my Lily and Carly, without my legs. How was I going to get by? I couldn't even afford the hospital bills. I wouldn't be able to pay the mortgage on my land. I said I was just going to be a burden on society, and that I would be better off dead."

"Yep, you were some kind of low that day, Tom," Parson Wesley said. "I tried to share with him how all we have in this life is simply lent to us, and that what is eternal is

"The word *charity* means love.
There are a lot of people in this town
who love you, whether you want them
to or not. And you can no more stop
their love for you than you can stop
the sun from rising in the east."

not something that can be signed over to a bank, but he wasn't much in the mood to listen."

"You were very kind in what you said to me, Parson. But no, I didn't really want to listen to you or anyone. I figured I would just go home and die there. Then, well, that's when miracles started happening.

"When they released me from the hospital, I asked if they would be sending me a bill. The head lady there just smiled. 'That's all been taken care of, Mr. Hayhurst,' she said. I figured she meant they were working with the insurance, and I would get a bill in the mail. I didn't know at the time that a collection had been taken up by the parson here, and all my medical bills were paid in full."

"Wow. That was really nice of—"

"That was just the beginning," Tom interrupted. "I got home here—Parson Wesley drove me himself—and saw my house had been painted. The gutters were fixed where they had been sagging. Inside of my house, all of my wife and daughter's clothing and personal things were gone, but their pictures and such were displayed in a very nice way, almost like a gallery of their lives. It felt like they were still with me. My kitchen was stocked with enough food to feed a city. There was an electric wheelchair for me, and the doorways had been enlarged so I could get around. Then I saw two envelopes on the table. The first was marked schedule—I opened it and saw that people were scheduled to be here with me around the clock. That was more than three years ago, and there has not been a day gone by when I have not had someone here with me."

Ryan was listening with rapt attention now. He had never heard of such generosity before. "And what was in the second envelope, Mr. Hayhurst?"

"It was simply labeled 'Paid In Full.' I opened it slowly and found the deed to my house and land inside. It was stamped 'Paid In Full' across the front. As I stared at it, your aunt and uncle came in.

"'Hayhurst,' James said, 'I know nothing can ever replace what you've lost, but we are doing what we can to see you don't lose any more. You'll never have to worry about making another payment on this place. It's yours.' He told me that a fund had been set up to pay the taxes and insurance. I said I couldn't take his charity like that. And you know what he said? 'The word *charity* means love. There are a lot of people in this town who love you, whether you want them to or not. And you can no more stop their love for you than you can stop the sun from rising in the east.'

"I continued to protest, because it's a lot harder for me to receive than it is to give. I kept feeling like I needed to do something to pay them back. Your aunt set me straight. 'Tom, you are doing us a great favor by allowing us to give to you and to serve you. It keeps us all from being focused on ourselves, which only produces lifeless, soulless people. You are giving us a chance to live the way God made for us to live.'

"I had to think on that a long time, but I finally came around to seeing what she meant. I still work, mind you. I was a teacher as well as a farmer, you know. I love to teach, so I tutor the young people around here in English and history and social studies, things like that. If they offer to pay me, I just tell them to give it to the parson. Although it sounds to me like he might need some tutoring from you, young man, on how to add up numbers the right way."

Ryan laughed. "Oh, he'll do till another comes around."

10

The parson drove Ryan to the Feed 'n Seed just in time to meet his uncle. James and Ryan climbed into the pickup for the ride back home. They passed the first few miles in silence, then James spoke up.

"Were you able to help the parson with his accounting?"

"Yes, sir," Ryan said. "It was a fairly easy problem to rectify. But then he said something that still has me puzzled. He wanted to introduce me to the richest man around."

"Ah, so you met old Tom Hayhurst, huh?"

"That's the problem. Don't get me wrong—Mr. Hayhurst is a nice man. And it's really nice what you and the others have done for him since his accident. But I don't see how he is so rich. Did he get a big insurance settlement? He certainly can't earn that much as a tutor."

James shook his head. "You just don't get it, son, do

you? All riches don't come with dollar signs attached. True riches can't be measured by bank accounts. Money is not the only sign of wealth. It's not even a very good one."

Ryan knew he was being reprimanded. He chose his next words carefully. "So how is it that you see Mr. Hayhurst's wealth, but I don't?"

"Because you have never learned what makes one truly wealthy. Ryan, I'm not one to go around preaching or quoting Bible verses, but there is one that I've pretty much got memorized. It's a saying of Jesus when he was talking to those just learning who he was and what he was all about. It goes like this:

"'Do not store up for yourselves treasures on earth, where moths and vermin destroy, and where thieves break in and steal. But store up for yourselves treasures in heaven, where moths and vermin do not destroy, and where thieves do not break in and steal. For where your treasure is, there your heart will be also.'*

"Tom cannot do for himself anymore because some drunk driver stole his wealth—his worldly wealth, that is. He had his ability to farm and teach and walk where

---

* Matthew 6:19–21.

he wanted to go taken from him. That's when he had to relearn what his treasure really was. His wife and daughter were his treasure. Now they are in heaven where no one can ever steal them from Tom. He loves them dearly to this day."

Ryan sat quietly thinking this through. It was a completely different way of picturing "treasure" for him. Something was gnawing away at his insides that he couldn't describe.

After a moment, James continued. "And Tom is allowing many of the rest of us to store up our treasure in heaven as well. When we give to Tom, we are becoming wealthy. It's in giving that a person truly accumulates what will last."

Ryan thought he saw a flaw in his uncle's presentation, and sought a way to redeem his reputation as someone who knew what wealth was. "But if you always give to someone and not let them earn their own way, well, won't that lead to that person taking advantage of you?"

James frowned. "There is a huge difference between 'taking' and 'receiving.' Someone who takes thinks only of themselves and shows no gratitude. You are right that this is a bad trait and unfortunately all too common today. But for someone like Tom who has learned to receive, the results are humility and gratitude, which are very good things to possess. But now I'm starting to sound like the parson."

They drove on in silence until they turned onto the road that led to the ranch. Then James found the words to conclude his sermon. "Ryan, you can sum up all of Tom Hayhurst's wealth in one word: *love*. While his wife and daughter were living, he loved them greatly. We all knew he did. He loves the children he teaches, even if he comes across as a gruff old man. And he is loved by young and old alike in this town. Although it was hard at first, Tom has come to learn to receive love that is given him. Love is what makes a person wealthy, Ryan. When you learn that, you will have learned all there is to know."

Ryan thought about what his uncle said. Yes, he could see that love was important, but was that really all there was to learn? Then were his years in college and graduate school wasted? He asked his uncle this question.

"Not wasted, no," Uncle James answered. "Education is very important, but too often we place all our emphasis on knowledge without adding wisdom. I'll bet you don't know the difference, do you?"

"You have to choose to live the life
you want on purpose—with purpose.
Otherwise life just happens,
and you'll look back at the end
and wonder what it was all about."

Ryan had learned by now not to try to out-think his uncle. "I'll bet you're going to tell me, Uncle James."

They had reached the house now. It faced the west, where the sun was beginning its journey beneath the horizon.

"Knowledge," James said as he and Ryan sat on the porch, "is gaining information. Wisdom is learning how to use that information in a way to help yourself and others. Too many people go to school, open their heads, and let teachers pour in knowledge. But they leave without ever gaining wisdom. They have no idea what to do with all that knowledge. They spend their lives thinking that making money is their purpose."

The sun broke through a cloud and shone its rays almost directly at Ryan. At the same time, something broke open inside of him, like a ray of light in his head. Two words danced in his mind: *love* and *purpose*.

"I suppose I don't know my purpose, Uncle James. I had thought all along it was to help my dad and one day take over the company as my own. At least that was the plan. Is that not a good purpose?"

"I want to be clear that there is nothing wrong with

making money. It's what we do with it and how we make it that matters. A famous preacher once said, 'Make all you can, save all you can, give all you can.' The labels on those 'cans' determine our purpose in life. If the only 'can' you fill is the 'make all you can,' that will make you one kind of person. If you focus on the 'give all you can,' then you are another kind of person. You have to choose to live the life you want on purpose—with purpose. Otherwise life just happens, and you'll look back at the end and wonder what it was all about.

"I have a purpose every morning. I want to serve my God, love my wife and son, and help those in need. In order to do this, some days I'm riding herd or branding calves or building a barn with my nephew. Other days the best way I can achieve my purpose is to sit still and appreciate the sunset. But I always have a purpose in mind, Ryan. And do you know what motivates my purpose each day?"

"Let me guess, Uncle James. Love?"

James chuckled. "Boy, you might make it yet."

11

*L*ove was not a word Ryan had ever thought much about, at least not in a long time. His mother told him he was much loved, but he seldom heard his father say "I love you," so he took it that love was something for women, while men focused on another four-letter word—*work*. For his uncle, a man whom Ryan admired as a strong male role model, to equate love with wealth gave Ryan a real jolt. What did love, an emotion, have to do with tangible assets like stocks and bonds and land and cash?

He lay awake that night with these thoughts tangled in his head. Just as he had one knot untied and was beginning to fall asleep, another knot emerged. What was life all about anyway? Was there really a purpose to anyone's existence other than to work, accumulate as much as possible, then retire to spend what you had made?

Would he never arrive but always scramble to learn more and more? And to what end? All he had learned thus far in his years in school apparently didn't amount to much. He wasn't doing the job he had studied for. He was swinging a lousy hammer! And not even doing that very well. Where was the wisdom in that?

And why did his father have to send him here in the first place? Ryan had different ideas about what it meant to become a man than his dad. Why couldn't he work it out on his own? Maybe he should go open his own transportation business in competition with his dad. That would show him that Ryan was a man.

In the midst of this thought, he finally drifted to a fitful sleep. He dreamed of trucks and horses and legs. Then he saw Kayla smiling at him. "Ryan, Ryan, Ryan," she said, laughing. "You need to wake up and smell the coffee."

"Ryan," he heard again. "Honey, it's after eight. Do you want to get up now?" It was the voice of Aunt Helena, and when Ryan forced one eye open, he saw her standing in the sunlit doorway.

He bolted upright and rubbed his eyes. "I'm sorry. I must have overslept. Tell Uncle James I'll be down as fast as I can get dressed."

"James has already left, honey. You're to take a day off. He said you earned it for helping the parson find his missing money. I have coffee for you downstairs when you are ready."

Ryan lay back down on the bed and mentally beat himself up for sleeping so long. Then he began to replay the thoughts he had the night before but stopped himself before the knots overtook him. He knew he would think better once he showered and got some coffee in him. The one thought he could not quite shake was the dream of the laughing Kayla. That thought went beyond his mind to his heart, and somehow that both scared him and made him feel alive in a way he had never known before.

After a quick breakfast and two cups of coffee, he asked Aunt Helena if she thought it would be okay for him to saddle Pony Boy and take him out for a while. Helena thought that an excellent idea, so Ryan went to the barn, fed Pony Boy an apple he had grabbed from the bowl on the kitchen table, then put on a blanket and saddle. He was just adjusting the cinch strap when Kayla walked in.

"Good job, Office Boy." Kayla lifted her chin. "It looks like you've been doing that all your life."

Ryan took in a satisfied breath. Maybe he was learning something after all. "I just thought I would take him out for a ride. Uncle James gave me the day off."

"Yep, Helena told me where you were. Mind if I amble alongside for a bit?"

As they rode, Ryan asked, "What will you call them, you know—James and Helena—once you and Hank get married?"

"Who said we were getting married?"

"Well, I guess I just figured, you know, since you guys have been going together for a long time that you would get married."

Kayla fidgeted with the reins. "What if I don't really love Hank? What if there was someone else who came along?" A question seemed to burn in her eyes. Did she mean she was falling in love with him?

They came to the top of a slight hill, with a view of the vast vista in front of them. Ryan halted his horse, and Kayla did the same. They sat there silently.

Two Ryans were sitting atop Pony Boy at that time. The first Ryan was the practical, MBA-earning, business-focused Ryan. This Ryan believed in goal-setting and, more importantly, goal-attaining. He was taught, both in school and by his father, to set his sights on what he wanted and then find a way to get it, no matter the cost to others. That was how "winners" operated, wasn't it? It was this Ryan who saw a crack in the relationship between Kayla and Hank. The win-at-all-costs Ryan wanted to exploit that, to capitalize on Kayla's weakness and get her to see that it was he, not Hank, she was meant for.

The second Ryan was like his mother, more sentimental and cozy. This Ryan wanted to hold Kayla, to make her feel at ease with him, to let her know she could count on him to understand her feelings and care for her. This Ryan wanted to bring her flowers and chocolates, to hold her hand and kiss her gently.

As these two Ryans wrestled, a third Ryan began to emerge. This was a new Ryan, born out of the weeks of working with his uncle, learning lessons not taught in schools. It was a Ryan that came from watching his aunt express love for her family and friends in extraordinary ways. A Ryan that took shape from what he learned—perhaps unlearned—about money from Parson Wesley. And a Ryan formed by the love he felt for this woman in front of him. But more than any of this, it was a Ryan that was brand new, and somehow he knew it was his friendship with Jesus that was making him feel this way. In the end, it was this new Ryan who spoke up.

"Kayla, these months I have spent here have been made so … special, I guess … in big part because of you. You make me feel ways I have never felt before with anyone. But …"

"Don't say it, Ryan. Don't say it—please."

"Kayla, I need to say this, for both of us. You are part of—of all this." He waved his hand toward the horizon. "But I'm not. Remember, I'm Office Boy. I was born to the city, to working in offices and pushing a pencil. You grew up breathing this air, seeing the mountains and the endless big sky. I drive trucks—you ride horses. Kayla, you belong here. And right now, I have no idea where I belong. I just know that you need to be here. And, well, Hank is my cousin. I have no right to take you from him. He needs you, Kayla. And I think you need him as well."

When he had finished, Ryan sat still in his saddle, gazing straight ahead toward the distant horizon. He could hear Kayla crying next to him, and he had to fight the urge to say he didn't mean what he said, that he would always be there for her. He started to reach out his hand toward her, but she stopped him.

"Let's go back. Hank'll be wondering where I am."

The rest of that day and in the days that followed, when Kayla spoke to Ryan at all, it was in a stiff, formal manner. And she constantly commented on Hank's character in only the most glowing manner. Even Hank noticed this. "I don't know what's gotten into that girl," he said. "But I kinda like it."

The following week, on Tuesday, Ryan had finished working with his uncle, showered, and changed into some clean clothes. He sat on the front porch, drinking a glass of iced tea and trying to work out if the clouds gathering to the west predicted bad weather or were just moving through when Kayla drove up in her pickup. She got out with her head down, not looking at Ryan, and made her way up the sidewalk. But when she reached the porch, instead of going straight inside as he expected her to, she sat down on

But more than any of this, it was
a Ryan that was brand new, and
somehow he knew it was his
friendship with Jesus that was making
him feel this way. In the end, it was
this new Ryan who spoke up.

a chair next to him. They sat in silence for several minutes before Ryan began to speak.

"No, let me talk first." She still stared at the painted porch floor. "I need to say something. Ryan, what you said the other day really hurt me. No, let me finish. Your words hurt because I put my heart out where it didn't belong. I had been flirting with you since you first got here, partly to get Hank's attention, but partly because I found you, well, a challenge. I wanted to try to change you into the person I wanted you to be. I know that is a very immature thing to do, but there you have it. I'm sorry I treated you like that. That was unkind of me."

"Kayla, you don't have to …"

"No, I'm on a roll, so let me keep going. Ryan, the other day you showed great courage in what you said. It showed that you, more than me, know what love is really supposed to look like. I'm not so dumb as to not know that you care for me, at least a little bit. I threw myself at you, and it would have been easy for you to catch me. But instead of doing the easy thing, you did the right thing. Yes, it was very courageous of you. And I have to think that your new Friend—Jesus—was helping you."

Ryan sat quietly for a moment, wondering if Kayla was now finished and would let him speak. But when he went to speak, all he could think to say was, "I love you, Kayla."

Her eyes rounded. "I know you do, Ryan. I think you are just now learning how to love, and I feel honored to be the recipient of your first real attempt. Oh, I don't mean that in a harsh way. I think it's wonderful the changes that are taking place in you. I only hope that I can someday learn to love as you are learning to."

They sat in silence for a while, watching the clouds darken and seeing flashes of lightning in the distance but not yet hearing the thunder.

Finally, Ryan spoke. "What happens now?"

"Now?" Kayla replied. "Now I go inside and tell Hank it's high time he asks me to marry him. You were right, you know. I do need him. And he certainly needs me. At least, I hope he does."

"And me?"

"You, Mr. Westcott, are destined for greatness. I'm not sure in what way. Somehow I don't think it's in the trucking business, but what do I know? I do know that your office with a window is going to seem awfully small compared with what you've got before you right now. Maybe we'll get out East some day and visit you." Kayla's sassiness was coming back. "Maybe you'll give me a ride in one of your big trucks."

"Maybe," Ryan said. "But only if you bring some of the big sky with you."

12

Dear Dad,
    The summer is coming to a close. Can I come home now?

Actually, I'm in no real hurry to leave here. There is something about the Montana sky and the mountains that gives me a peace I haven't known before.

I haven't been just lying around, admiring the scenery though. Uncle James and I finished his barn this week. I never knew how much fun hard work like that could be. Well, it wasn't all fun. It was mostly just hard. But at the end of each day, we had accomplished something you could see, and that was really satisfying. Now the barn is up and ready to be used. Uncle James and Aunt Helena plan to use it as more of a community gathering spot than to hold animals or hay. Uncle James said, "What the world needs is more dancing," and Aunt Helena said, "Then you need to learn to dance so my toes don't get stepped on." They are a really great couple, Dad. Watching them has led me to learn what love looks like.

I've actually learned a lot this summer while being here. Did I learn enough to come back and work for you? I don't know. I'll have to leave that up to you. All I know is I'm not the same as when I last saw you. I feel different in a good way.

If I had to sum up what has made me feel this way, I would say I have learned seven things. Or maybe it would be better to say what I've learned fits into seven categories. I'll try my best to write what I mean, but it's kind of hard to put into words. I've always been more of a numbers guy, but I'll try to use words to say what I'm thinking.

First of all, I've learned about taking care of my body. We all need to get our bodies in their natural rhythms, just like the soil. We experience winter, spring, summer, and fall every day in our bodies, and if we don't respect that, then we cannot function as we are meant to. For instance, winter is when we sleep so our bodies can recover. But winter must give way to spring—meaning we can't sleep until noon or we will have missed spring. We can't jump from winter to summer and expect to be productive. I know this may be hard to understand the way I'm explaining it, and I'm not doing a good job saying it, but I can say I feel like I have a lot more energy and I enjoy each day a lot more now that I am trying to stay in rhythm.

I found that eating the proper food at the proper time makes me feel better. I've been eating "real" food, Dad. Aunt Helena is a great cook, but the meals are simple meat-and-potatoes kinds of things. They grow a lot of their own vegetables and get other foods from neighbors who grow other things. There is a real pleasure in eating something you helped to grow and harvest. I used to think of mealtime as something to hurry through or skip altogether. Now I see it as the best time of day. We relax and enjoy what we are eating. I have learned to eat less and enjoy it more. Again, Dad, maybe this doesn't make sense the way I'm writing it right now. I'll try to show you when I get home. Maybe I'll even cook you an old-fashioned ranch supper.

The second thing I learned was relationships with others mean more than anything, but they take a lot of work.

It's just like the barn we built. If we had not put forth the effort to make sure all the pieces fit correctly and as they should, then it wouldn't last very long. As a matter of fact, making the barn strong started long before we ever hammered a nail. (More about hammering in a minute.) Uncle James bought a bunch of old wood that had been a barn in Pennsylvania. At first I thought he must have made a mistake. I thought he should have bought new boards instead of using old ones. But he said the old ones had been through seasons of hot and cold, drought and floods, and were stronger for it. That made me think about marriage and how a husband and wife need to endure the hard times so they can become strong.

A key to having good relationships is putting others ahead of myself. I see that in Uncle James and Aunt Helena. It's almost like they have a daily contest to see who can out-give the other! Hank, on the other hand, has a long way to go in that area, and he almost lost his girl because of it. Kayla is a wonderful girl, Dad, even if Hank has trouble seeing that. She and I grew pretty close, so close that I think she would have left Hank for me. I had to do something really hard, but something I believe was the right thing to

"I learned that I need to keep learning, and that pride keeps me from continuing to learn and improve myself. I had to become humble and accept that I don't know everything."

do, and that's not try to take her away from Hank. He is my cousin, after all, even if he is kind of blind when it comes to love. But it felt kind of, I don't know, freeing to do what I knew was the right thing to do and put Hank and Kayla ahead of my own desires.

The third thing I learned was that one should never stop learning. That's where the hammer comes in. Did you know there are more than ten kinds of hammers? And that there is a right and wrong way to hammer a nail? I learned the wrong way the hard way—my thumb still hurts! What really hurt, though, was my pride. I learned that I need to keep learning, and that pride keeps me from continuing to learn and improve myself. I had to become humble and accept that I don't know everything. I learned that the hard way when I got on top of a horse! But once I accepted that I didn't know how to ride properly, I began to learn. Now I can get in and out of the saddle pretty well. And once I realized that I don't know everything, learning actually became a challenge.

The fourth lesson learned is similar to the third. Uncle James taught me the difference between knowledge and wisdom. I gained a lot of knowledge during my years in school, and while that was a good start, it takes wisdom to give knowledge power. I'm very thankful for the education I got, Dad—and I am so grateful for you paying for it all—but I thought that learning stopped when we tossed our hats in the air. In reality, what I needed to learn was how to learn, so I can keep learning the rest of my life. Things change all the time, Dad, and only those who have gained both knowledge and wisdom can make sense of this world and know their place in it.

I don't want it to sound like Uncle James and I just sat and talked all the time. We worked hard every day! (If you're counting, Dad, "work" is the fifth lesson I learned.) At first, I wasn't really used to working like we did. I remember when I was an undergrad and went on a spring break trip with the marketing club to Belize to help build a home for abused women. There were twelve of us, and we would work until noon, then play the rest of the day and night. I guess that is how I pictured working with Uncle James. No way. We started before the sun was up, and we were still working when Aunt Helena called us for dinner. Most nights I went to bed around eight, bone-tired. But it was a good tired, as people say. I didn't know hard work

"I discovered a whole new meaning
to wealth. One that doesn't
necessarily involve money.
I met a man who measures his wealth
by the number of people who care
for him and stores up his treasure
where no one will ever be able
to steal it from him."

could be so satisfying, but it is. And believe me, on a ranch like this, there is always work to do. And now when I view the barn we built, I feel a sense of great accomplishment, and it makes me want to build something else.

Uncle James taught me the importance of rest as well (going back to having our bodies in a rhythm). We never worked after dinner if we could help it (although things happen), and Sunday was a day of rest. On Sundays we would go visit other ranches for a cookout, or ride horses, or just sit on the front porch and wait for others to come visit us. It wasn't a lazy day. It was a good reward for a good week's work.

Okay, where am I? Oh—number six. Dad, you have built a strong business that brings in a lot of money, and with that money you supply jobs for many others who then can use that money to support their families and buy things that keep others in business. That's the nature of capitalism, and I think that is the best economic system we could have. But, and I don't want you to take this wrong, I discovered a whole new meaning to wealth. One that doesn't necessarily involve money. I met a man who measures his wealth by the number of people who care for him and stores up his treasure where no one will ever be able to steal it from him. I know this probably doesn't make sense the way I'm explaining it, but it has made a profound impact on my life. Now I see the making and saving of money with a different purpose in mind. As a matter of fact, my whole life seems to have taken on a new purpose.

And that brings me to my final point, lesson number seven. I don't know any better way to say it than this: I met God. Kayla helped me to see that Jesus is real, not just some religious figure from the past, and that he wants to be my friend. Now Dad, don't freak out. I'm not going to become a preacher or anything. At least I don't think I am. (Hmmm … I never actually thought about it until just now.) But I do know that I have a new outlook on life now. And I feel like a different person, knowing that the God who made these mountains and this beautiful land wants to hang out with me.

I've learned a lot this summer, Dad. Am I a man now? Well, I think I can say that I am now on the right path. Before I was like a horse that just wanders around, but now, well, God has put a bridle on me and is directing me the way I should go. I feel like there is a purpose in every day. And I suppose that makes me a man-in-training. I have a feeling I'll be in training the rest of my life, and that's okay.

I'm going to hate to leave here, Dad. But I think it's time I come home. I'll call you when I have my ticket so you'll know when to pick me up.

I've missed you, Dad. And by the way—I think you are a wonderful father. If not before now, certainly in how you were courageous and wise enough to send me here for the summer. Thank you, Dad. Thank you.

Love,
Ryan

13

A year to the day after Ryan returned home, Ryan's dad invited him to dinner at the same Italian bistro where he had banished Ryan to the mountains. Ryan could sense that his father had something big on his mind.

"Dad, I feel kind of funny eating here with you. You're not going to send me away again, are you? Like, to South America or something?"

His dad forked a bite of manicotti. "No, Ryan. Not this time. But I do have something I want to talk with you about. And this time, I want to talk man-to-man. Ryan, I've seen a huge change in you since you returned from your uncle's place. A change I was hoping to see, but more than that. I sent you away to learn to become a man, and you have surpassed my greatest hopes. So much so that …" He looked away.

Ryan spoke up. "So much so that what, Dad?"

"So much so that I wonder if I am the one who now needs to learn how to be a man. Ryan, can I share something with you? You've now got me longing to visit the West, to see this big sky you keep talking about, to, well, maybe learn to ride a horse. Do you think I could ride one?"

Ryan laughed out loud. "Dad, if I can learn, anyone can! But let me tell you right now—don't pull the reins too tight if you don't want to go flying!"

They both laughed for a while, and Ryan relished the father-son bond that had been growing since he returned.

Finally, Dad collected himself. "You've gotten me thinking. Let me just share my thoughts with you, and you can then shoot holes in them. What if we—you and I—were to move to Montana, buy a ranch out there? What if we were to then invite young men out to this ranch to teach them the things you learned? Do you think such a thing could work?"

Ryan jumped up from his seat and raised his hands into the air as if his Nittany Lions had just scored a touchdown. The others seated in the restaurant peered at him for a moment and then went back to their dinners with one eye on this crazy person. "That's the craziest idea I've ever heard." Ryan sat back down. "When do we start?"

Ryan gazed up at the big sky,
now dotted with clouds. He never
tired of the sky or the mountains—
and he never stopped being grateful
that his father loved him enough
to send him here in the first place.

Things fell together quickly after that. Ryan's dad sold his business with a sizable amount upfront and structured payments going forward. Along with the sale of their house, PJ and Ryan purchased one hundred and sixty acres of land adjacent to James Royale's King Ranch. James and Helena seemed very glad to have PJ and Ryan as neighbors and even helped build and plan their ranch for teaching others to live a life on purpose, though James first said, "You notice Ryan didn't get no diploma. He's just started his learning." Helena responded, "And you ain't got no diploma either, you old cowboy."

Two years later, Ryan and his dad finished their work for the day, and Ryan popped into the kitchen to ask Frieda, their cook and housekeeper, to prepare some drinks. When he came back into the living room, Hank and Kayla were seated on the couch. His dad rocked in a chair, holding a three-month-old baby.

"Howdy, Ryan," Hank said. "Could I trouble you for a . . ."

"Coming right up, Hank. A frosty cold one. And iced tea for you, Kayla. I suppose Skye has already had his drink?"

Kayla nodded. "That he has, Ryan. And if Uncle PJ doesn't stop bouncing him up and down like that, he's going to see Skye's lunch all over his shirt."

Ryan's dad heard what she said and stopped Skye in mid-bounce. He cradled him in his arms instead. "I've been meaning to ask you. Why Skye?" he asked as he made faces at the little one. "How did you come up with that name?"

"Well, you can blame Ryan for that," Hank said. "He was always yammerin' on about how big the sky is here and all, so …"

"And then Ryan met Someone who is bigger than the biggest sky. And we wanted our son to get a good start in meeting that Someone himself, so, well, Skye."

They were just settling in with their drinks when they heard more vehicles coming down the drive.

"That'll be your horses, Ryan," Hank said. "Eight geldings, per your order. We can go into town tomorrow to order the tack you'll need."

"They'll make good company for Pony Boy," Ryan said. "Let's go look 'em over, Hank."

As they walked to the truck, Ryan gazed up at the big sky, now dotted with clouds. He never tired of the sky or the mountains—and he never stopped being grateful that his father loved him enough to send him here in the first place.

The End … But Really, Just the Beginning

The Rancher's Guide to Living Life on Purpose

*W*e can't all go spend the summer working a ranch in Montana to discover what it means to live life on purpose. But we can begin today the process of discovery, and the guide that follows can not only begin to help you identify what it means to live a life of purpose, but it can also be the beginning of a brand new you as you find a purpose in living.

Take a day to get away by yourself; go to the mountains, a park, a quiet place in a coffee bar where you can think, reflect, and pray. Take only a pad of paper and try to disconnect from electronics for one day. Also bring a book or two that have impacted your life. One of those should be a Bible, if you have one. You know the rancher would say to take it.**

Reflect on the questions and exercises that follow.

** The author wishes to acknowledge Building Champions and Daniel Harkavy for introducing this rancher, two decades ago, to finding purpose in living by using this guide to discovery. While I've adapted the guide on these pages over the years and tweaked it again for *The Rancher's Gift*, I want to acknowledge and thank Building Champions for first introducing me to this content.

Take a day to get away by yourself;
go to the mountains, a park, a quiet
place in a coffee shop where you
can think, reflect, and pray.

1. **As Ryan's dad PJ did for his son, ask your-self, where are you in life today and where do you want to be?**

   a. Those closest to me would say about me ...

   b. What I would say about me and where I am today ...

   c. Who do you want to be remembered by?

   d. What do you want to be remembered for?

2. As summer ended, James had shared these
   seven areas or categories in life to find
   purpose. Think about the areas of your life
   that are important. They may be the same,
   or you may want to add one or two more.

   1) Health – taking care of your body

   2) Relationships – family and friends

   3) Never stop learning – self-development

   4) Knowledge – gain wisdom by having a mentor

   5) Work – career, leading, serving

   6) Money – finance, charity

   7) Spiritual –a relationship with Jesus, Creator of
      the mountains and life

Areas of your life that you might consider:

God	Spouse
Children	Health
Finance	Career
Family	Self-development
Friends	Vacation
Fun	Charity
Community	My dream

3. **As the rancher would say, the sun is coming up, let's get to work.**

Now that you have identified the categories
you want to find purpose in, take time to think
and write about where you want to be in
each twenty or thirty years from now. Picture
yourself on the ranch porch looking at the
Rockies or in front of your fireplace. You're now
sixty-five and looking back or seventy-five and
looking back. What choices did you make today
that allow you to look back and see a life lived
on purpose, with purpose?

4. Let's refine your purpose.

What is your purpose in each of the identified categories? What one sentence would clearly define the result you desire. Then in the space provided or on your notepad write your purpose for each.

5. There is a life to live on purpose. Up and at 'em!

Just like building a barn, Ryan would remind you that plans are good but action is required. Take the time now to write what actions you will begin doing today so when you look back at sixty-five, you'll know you lived a life on purpose.

Get up in the morning, and as Ryan learned during his summer at the ranch, you must remember these are your life priorities! What will you do daily, weekly, monthly, quarterly, or annually in each category? You need to be able to schedule and track your progress and success. What you establish must be quantifiable and measurable and reviewed daily and weekly.

6. Don't wander.

Find a partner—a Ryan, a Kayla, a James, a
Helena—who will hold you accountable in the
categories of your life that you've said are most
important. You will then stay the course and
not wander away from the joy and freedom of
living a life on purpose.

ABOUT THE AUTHORS

Dennis Worden, founder of Worden Associates, is known as a motivated, visionary leader. He's an outstanding communicator, encouraging individuals and organizations to press beyond mediocrity, rise to excellence, and live life on purpose. A rancher at heart, having lived in Montana, New Mexico, and Oklahoma, Dennis and his wife, Gayle, their three daughters husbands, and ten grandkids now live in Atlanta, Georgia.

Jeff Dunn lives and works in Tulsa, Oklahoma. He and his wife, Kathy, have three children and five grandchildren. He writes books, articles, and blogs. and reads everything he can get his hands on.

START LIVING
A LIFE ON PURPOSE

- Access additional life-planning tools
- Share your own experiences
- Develop a personal and professional life plan with our coaching resources
- Give feedback to the authors
- Arrange for Dennis to speak to your group
- Help spread the word about living a life on purpose!

www.TheRanchersGift.com

info@TheRanchersGift.com